DRAGON STORM
TOM AND IRONSKIN

Alastair Chisholm

illustrated by Eric Deschamps

A STEPPING STONE BOOK™

Random House 🏠 New York

Meet the next Dragonseer:

CARA AND SILVERTHIEF

Coming soon:

ELLIS AND PATHSEEKER
MIRA AND FLAMETELLER

CONTENTS

Text copyright © 2022 by Alastair Chisholm
Cover art and interior illustrations copyright © 2022 by Eric Deschamps

All rights reserved. Published in the United States by Random House Children's Books, a division of Penguin Random House LLC, New York. Originally published in paperback in slightly different form in the United Kingdom by Nosy Crow, Ltd, London, in 2022.

Random House and the colophon are registered trademarks and A Stepping Stone Book and the colophon are trademarks of Penguin Random House LLC.

Visit us on the Web!
rhcbooks.com

Educators and librarians, for a variety of teaching tools, visit us at
RHTeachersLibrarians.com

Library of Congress Cataloging-in-Publication Data
Names: Chisholm, Alastair (Children's author), author. | Deschamps, Eric (Artist), illustrator.
Title: Tom and Ironskin / Alastair Chisholm; illustrated by Eric Deschamps.
Description: First American edition. | New York: Random House Children's Books, [2022] | Series: Dragon storm; 1 | Summary: "Tom discovers that he is a legendary dragonseer—a person who can summon a dragon—but he's not sure he's a true dragonseer, especially when he has trouble summoning his dragon, Ironskin."
—Provided by publisher.
Identifiers: LCCN 2021042250 (print) | LCCN 2021042251 (ebook) |
ISBN 978-0-593-47954-4 (paperback) | ISBN 978-0-593-47955-1 (library binding) |
ISBN 978-0-593-47956-8 (ebook)
Subjects: CYAC: Fantasy. | Dragons—Fiction. | LCGFT: Fantasy fiction.
Classification: LCC PZ7.1.C5166 To 2022 (print) | LCC PZ7.1.C5166 (ebook) |
DDC [Fic]—dc23

Printed in the United States of America
10 9 8 7 6 5 4 3 2 1
First American Edition

In the land of Draconis, there are no dragons.

Once, there were. Once, humans
and dragons were friends and guarded
the land. They were wise, and strong, and
created the great city of Rivven together.

But then came the Dragon Storm, and the
dragons retreated from the world
of humans. To the men and women of
Draconis, they became legend and myth.

And so, these days, in the land of Draconis,
there are no dragons. . . .

Or so people thought.

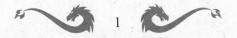

1
TOMÁS

Tom worked the bellows, blowing air into the fire until it glowed a fierce yellow. Beside him, his dad hammered at a long piece of metal. He moved quickly, holding the piece in a pair of pincers. Sparks flew with every clang.

"Ready, Tomás?" he roared.

"Yes!" shouted Tom.

Dad plunged the metal into the fire, ignoring the spitting flames. He kept it

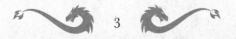

there until it softened. When he removed it, the metal gleamed orange. He hammered again at the edges until it was the shape of a sword.

Tom gasped in the heat.

"Get ready!" Dad warned. He lifted the sword and sank it deep into a water trough. There was a ferocious HISSSSSS! Steam filled the room, and the water bubbled and spat. He pulled the sword out and placed it on the rack beside the fire.

"There," he said, wiping his forehead. "We'll let that temper, and then it will be ready to polish. Good work, son."

Tom grinned. His face was hot and his arms ached, but he loved helping in the smithy. He loved working the forge, and the way he and Dad turned lumps of ugly metal into tools, or horseshoes, or swords. Now Dad looked at the rack, where eight swords lay ready, and nodded in approval.

"Time for lunch."

Dad prepared some food and Tom laid the table, finishing just as Mom arrived from the marketplace.

"Goodness, look at you!" she scolded. "Covered in soot in my lovely kitchen! Shoo!"

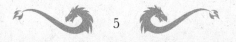

"Sorry!" said Dad. "Come on, let's get cleaned up." He squeezed past Mom, giving her a big kiss and smearing soot over her face.

She spluttered. "Out! Out, or you'll be eating with the pig!"

Laughing, they went to the water pump to wash, then came back and sat down.

"How was the marketplace?" asked Dad, taking a large bite from a huge piece of bread.

Mom sighed. "Quiet. King Godfic has raised the grain tax again. Mildred Foxton says it's because of dragons burning the crops."

Dad grunted. "Maybe he just wants more money to add another tower to his palace."

"Shush," said Mom, glancing at Tom. "Keep that talk to yourself, Felipe."

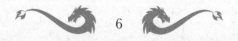

Dad glowered but said nothing.

Tom said, "Are there really dragons?"

Dad sighed. "A long time ago," he said. "They were all over the kingdom, and here in Rivven, too."

"They were terrible," said Mom. "Enormous! And they breathed fire! It was a wild time."

"But that was centuries ago," said Dad. "There hasn't been a dragon in Rivven for a thousand years."

Tom frowned. "If there aren't any dragons, then why do we make dragonswords?"

"The king insists, in case they ever come back." Dad shrugged. "Which is good news for us! Business is poor. The gold from this order will pay for food until spring comes."

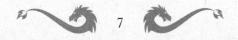

He finished his lunch.

"Let's push on, Tomás. Captain Hork wants to collect the swords tomorrow."

The forge had cooled, but after walking in the chilly winter air outside, it still seemed incredibly hot. Dad brought the swords down from the rack. They were black, with rough edges. Tom and Dad got to work.

Tom sharpened the blades with a special grinding stone that spat sparks, scraping away the rough edges until the swords were smooth and sharp. The metal had a strange, swirling pattern, like oil. Dad said it was because

of the secret ingredients he mixed into the ore, making them not just any swords but *dragon*swords, able to cut through a dragon's hide.

Tom placed each sword carefully back on the rack. But as he reached for the last one, he glanced at the forge—and gasped!

There was a face in the fire!

A face hung in the flames like a shadow, dark and shimmering. It wasn't human; it was longer, and bony, with a crest at the top of its head, and its eyes were two circles of fire.

Tom gazed at it as if in a dream. The eyes burned! Its mouth opened and showed rows of sharp, vicious teeth.

"Tomássssssss," it hissed.

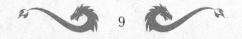

DRAGON STORM

Tom's mouth fell open.

"Be ready, Tomásssssssss. . . ."

"Tomás! Tom, what are you doing?"

Tom blinked and looked up. Dad was frowning at him.

"Are you all right, Tom?"

"I—I thought . . ." Tom peered into the fiery forge, but there was nothing there. "I thought I saw something," he muttered.

Dad smiled. "It's been a long day. Let's finish tomorrow."

Tom nodded, and they went in for supper.

That evening, tucked into his tiny bunk, he thought again about the face. The bony head. The sharp teeth. And the eyes . . .

He woke in the dark with a start. Then he laughed to himself at his imagination and went back to sleep.

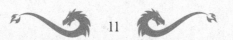

They finished the last sword the next morning. Tom checked the flames several times, but today there was nothing—just crackling wood and white-hot charcoal.

He held up the sword, watching it glitter.

Dad inspected it. "Good job, Tom. Let's finish up. Captain Hork will be here soon."

They packed the swords into crates by the doorway. But as Dad left, Tom looked again at the fire—and the face was there! Unmistakable, dark and fierce, with eyes of flame . . .

"Be ready, Tomásssss," it hissed. "He's here. . . ."

"Tomás!" bellowed Dad. "Come on, he's here!"

2
CAPTAIN HORK

"He's here!" bellowed Dad again. "Tomás?"

Tom jumped. He looked back at the forge, but the face had disappeared. What was happening? He shook his head and hurried out into the yard, where Captain Hork was waiting.

Captain Hork was the head of the King's Guard. He wore a ceremonial breastplate, a purple tunic that bulged over his waist, and

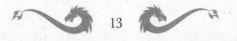

a helmet with a tall red plume. His face was
pink and sweaty, and he seemed displeased.
He was sitting on a thin brown horse whose
breath steamed in the cold air. Two soldiers
and a slim, young man, dressed all in black,
stood beside him.

Dad stepped forward. "Good morning—"

"Where are my swords?" interrupted Hork.
He had a loud, braying voice, like an angry
sheep.

Dad bowed. "They're here, sire." Tom could
tell Dad was annoyed but trying not to show it.

Tom fetched the crates, but Hork held up a
hand.

"I will inspect them first," he barked. "This

is King Godfic's money, you know—we won't pay for any old rubbish."

Dad's eyes glittered. "Yes, sire."

Hork clambered down from his horse, his large bottom swinging as he staggered to the ground. "Show me."

Tom unpacked a sword. But as he did so, he felt a strange sensation. It was as if he could see the face from the fire again, but in his mind now. It seemed to float in front of him. The sword handle suddenly felt unpleasant, almost clammy. And the oily pattern on its blade seemed sinister and slithery, like, like—

"Come on, boy!" snapped Hork.

Tom blinked and handed the sword over.

Hork gave it some practice sweeps, one so wild that he almost fell. Behind him, the soldiers grinned at each other.

Captain Hork frowned. "I'm not sure," he muttered. "They're very flimsy. . . ." He turned to Tom. "Take out another sword. Let me see you fight."

"Sire!" exclaimed Dad, then bit his lip. "Please . . . be careful."

"Oh, don't worry!" chuckled Hork. "I'm an expert. I won't harm the boy."

Dad sighed and nodded. Tom unpacked another sword. It felt wrong too.

"Come on, then!" said Hork.

Tom raised the sword, and immediately Hork lunged. Tom dodged, shifting his feet, keeping his balance. Hork gave a huge swing. Tom caught the blade against his, and they clanged. The swords were well balanced, light and strong. Tom parried, and Hork stumbled backward. He cursed as his helmet snapped shut. Captain Hork wasn't a very good swordsman.

Hork lunged again, and Tom blocked. But as he did so, he glanced at the oily pattern, moving and swirling. It was a snake! A snake, hissing and coiling around the blade! The face in his mind roared.

Tom dropped the sword in shock, and it clattered to the ground. Captain Hork attacked, pressing his blade against Tom's chest. "Yield, boy! Yield!"

Dad shouted, "He yields, sire!"

Hork stepped back, breathing heavily. "Yes!" he laughed. "My victory!"

Tom ignored him and stared at the sword. It looked normal again. There was no snake. Just a sword, like hundreds he'd helped to make. But suddenly he hated it. Even the thought

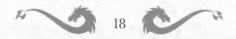

of touching it was horrible. As he packed it away, it seemed to twitch in his hand, and he shuddered.

"Well," said Hork, "they'll do, I suppose. Malik!"

The slim man in black stepped forward to hand Captain Hork a leather pouch. Hork tossed it to Dad.

Dad measured the weight and frowned. He counted the little gold pieces.

"This isn't enough," he said.

Hork shrugged. "The rate changed."

"But we agreed on a price!" exclaimed Dad.

The two soldiers helped Hork onto his horse. "Consider yourself grateful for the

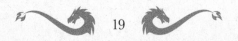

king's business, blacksmith," he warned with a sneer. "Understand?"

The muscles on Dad's shoulders bunched. He stepped forward suddenly. Captain Hork yelped and jerked back in fright. His horse skittered and started down the hill.

"Whoa!" he squawked. "Well, I'm, ah, leaving now. Whoa!" The horse kept going. "Whoa! Whoa, you brainless animal!"

Hork's horse cantered away. The two soldiers glanced at one another. Then each lifted a crate and followed after Hork. The slim man, Malik, started to leave too. But at the last moment, he turned and gazed at Tom, an odd expression on his face. . . .

Then he left.

TOM AND IRONSKIN

That evening, Tom and his parents ate supper in silence. Tom knew Mom and Dad were worried about money, and Tom was thinking about the face in the fire.

What was happening? First the face in the fire and then the strangeness with the swords. After Hork had left, Tom returned to the smithy and tried the other swords his dad had made, but they felt fine. Only the dragonswords seemed wrong.

There was a knock at the door, and Dad answered it.

It was the young man, Malik. He wore a dark cloak, wrapped tight around him.

"Good evening," he said. "I wondered if I might have a word."

Dad frowned. "What about?" he asked cautiously.

"I have an opportunity," said Malik. "One that might help your family."

He smiled and glanced at Tom.

"It is about your son."

3
MALIK

Malik sat at the table, in Tom's chair, and Dad poured him a mug of ale. Tom stood in the corner of their tiny room and watched him. Malik was young, with quick, clever eyes. A long, faded scar trailed down one side of his face.

"I wanted to apologize for Captain Hork's behavior today," he said.

Dad said nothing.

"I was impressed with your son," Malik continued, and Tom blinked in surprise. "Tell me, can he read and write?"

"Yes, sir," said Mom. "And do sums. He's a bright boy."

"How old is he?"

"Eleven."

Malik nodded. "The law says that every child must start to learn a trade by the age of twelve. What are your plans?"

"He'll work in the smithy with me," said Dad. "If he wants."

Malik tapped the table with his mug, as if thinking.

"I am a clerk," he said. "An assistant

to the king. I'm looking for an apprentice. I'd like to offer your son a place."

What? Tom thought.

"Sir," said Mom, astonished. "Tomás has no formal training—"

Malik waved a hand. "Oh, don't worry about that." He flicked a quick grin at Tom. "He'll stay at the dorms with the other apprentices, over on Parchment Lane. He'll work for me, and I'll train him." Malik smiled. "In five years he'll be a member of the Guild of Clerks."

"Oh, Felipe!" gasped Mom. She clutched Dad's arm. "A clerk!"

Dad nodded. His face was serious, but Tom knew he was stunned.

Clerks were very important people in

Rivven. They worked for the king, copying documents, writing contracts. They were gentry. They were rich. It was a world Tom could hardly imagine. He did enjoy writing. This was all so incredible!

Malik talked for a little longer and then left, promising to return tomorrow. After he'd gone, Tom's parents stared at each other.

"Well!" said Mom, delighted. She turned to Tom. "Imagine that!"

Tom nodded.

Dad noticed his expression. "What's wrong?"

Tom hesitated. "I like the smithy," he said.

Dad smiled. "I know. But . . . blacksmithing is a hard life. Money's tight these days. We

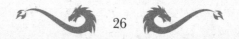

barely make enough to get by. Thin soup, straw beds . . . You're a good worker. You'd be a good smith. But you're clever too, like your mom. We always wanted better for you. This could change your life."

"Malik says you can try it out for a month," said Mom. "If you don't like it, you can come back." She hugged him. "You decide."

They went to bed and Tom lay awake in the dark. He should be excited, he knew. But . . . he thought of the face in the fire, warning him. *Be ready. He's here.* Tom didn't know why, but he had the strangest feeling, as if . . .

As if Malik wasn't telling them the truth.

Malik returned the next afternoon with a contract, a long black quill, and a pot of ink. Dad signed, then Mom, and finally Tom.

"There," said Malik, smiling at Tom. "That's settled."

There wasn't much to pack. Everything Tom owned fit into a small sack. Mom packed him a honey cake, and Dad gave him a sharp folding knife.

"You'll do well, son," he said. "I'm proud of you." He gathered Tom up into his enormous arms and hugged him hard.

"Look after yourself," said Mom. "Remember, we love you." And she hugged him too.

Then Malik and Tom set off. It was another cold day, and steam rose from their breath as they walked. Tom didn't look back. He felt that if he did, he might run all the way home. Instead, they followed the lane eastward, until Rivven's city center lay before them.

It was an impressive sight. Rivven was a large city. At its heart, a huge, rocky hill rose through like a crown. Houses and streets piled around each other at the base, in tiny twisting lanes. Woodsmoke rose from chimneys, drifting upward in the calm afternoon air. And from the top of the hill, King Godfic's palace, with its mighty walls and towers, glared down at them all.

As they walked, the last sunlight dripped away. The crowd bustled around them. People lit torches and fires. Someone played a fiddle from inside a pub. A man with a wagon of hay was arguing with a lamplighter, and a woman sold bread from a stall. But Malik led Tom away from the crowds, down a narrow lane, into the dark.

"You did well yesterday," he said.

Tom looked up. "Sir?"

"With Captain Hork." Malik grinned. "He's a fool, isn't he?"

Tom ducked his head. "Don't know, sir."

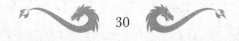

Malik nodded. "Those dragonswords. You helped your father make them?"

"Yes, sir."

"Hardly anyone knows how to make them anymore," said Malik. "Most are fakes. But those ones are real. Real . . . dragon killers, eh?"

Tom didn't answer. He glanced around the deserted lane. Malik said quietly, "You know they're real, don't you? You can feel them."

The hairs on the back of Tom's neck rose.

"Sir?"

"Tell me"—Malik's eyes glinted—"when did you see the face in the fire?"

Tom froze.

Malik chuckled. "Oh, yes, we know about the face in the fire. We've been looking for you, Tomás."

Tom stared at him. He stepped back. Malik frowned and reached for him.

A blinding white light suddenly blazed around them.

4

AN OFFER

"Argh!"

Tom staggered, almost fell. There was
white light everywhere, brilliant and blinding,
shining from something in front of him.

"Don't run!" Malik grabbed his arm.

"Let go!" shouted Tom, but Malik's grip was
like iron.

Tom screwed his eyes up. He could make
out a shape—a woman? Yes, a tall woman,

holding a staff. She waved one hand and the light disappeared. Now the world was dark. But just for a moment, Tom thought he'd seen something else behind her, a shadow moving. . . .

"Hello, Tomás," said the woman. "I'm sorry if we frightened you."

Her voice sounded old, but as clear and sharp as glass. "We've been looking for you. Do you know why?"

Tom shook his head.

"Because you've seen the face in the fire. Am I right?"

He shook his head again and tried to break free.

The woman peered at him and nodded.

"Yes, you've seen it. Perhaps it looked a little like this?"

And behind her, the dark shape moved.

It curled upward, uncoiling and stretching, enormous! Tom could make out thick black scales, a long neck, glinting claws, and a huge, bony head. . . .

A DRAGON.

Tom gasped. A dragon! It was a dragon!

"Don't be scared," murmured Malik.

But it's a dragon! thought Tom. And yet, strangely, he wasn't scared. He should be terrified! But . . .

The creature leaned forward. Its face was like the one Tom had seen, but dark midnight blue, with large yellow eyes. Its head was as wide as Tom's shoulders, its mouth full of razor-sharp white teeth. Tom felt its breath on his face! It was like warm mist, steaming in the icy air. . . .

"Good evening, Tomás," it said in a rich, deep voice. "My name is Angus."

Tom blinked. The dragon's lips pulled back,

revealing more teeth. After a second, Tom realized it was smiling.

"Um," he managed. "Um . . . hello?"

The dragon—Angus—tilted his head.

Malik released Tom's arm. "Touch him," he said quietly. "It's all right."

Tom considered running. But instead, very slowly, he reached forward and touched the dragon's snout.

It was like a dog's nose. It was warm, dry, and rough in a way that felt nice. Tom found himself stroking it, and the creature's eyes closed. He breathed out a puff of warm air. Then he nodded and pulled back into the shadows, leaving Tom staring after him.

"Tell me, Tomás," said the woman. "What do you know about dragons?"

Tom dragged his eyes away and tried to think. "Um, I don't . . . They're, ah, monsters, Mom says. They set fire to things. And they, um . . ." He stopped. *They eat people!* he wanted to say. But Angus was still watching him, and it seemed rude.

Tom cleared his throat. "And they're all gone. I mean . . ."

There hasn't been a dragon in Rivven for a thousand years, Dad had said.

The dragon hissed, as if laughing.

"Not all gone," said the woman. "But there are very few left. And they're not monsters.

Dragons are the most heroic creatures ever born."

She shook her head. "Once, there were many dragons. They helped to build this city and protect the land. We invited them from their world to ours, and we lived together in peace. Beside every dragon, there was a dragonseer. A human, Tomás. Someone with a special gift, who could see things beyond our world." She smiled. "Like a face in the fire."

Tom gaped at her. "What?"

"I saw you with the dragonswords," said Malik. "You could hardly bear to touch them. And I could tell just by looking at you. It changes someone when they see their dragon."

Tom gasped. "My dragon?"

The woman nodded. In Tom's mind, he saw the face in the fire smile. *Be ready.* . . .

"We're here to offer you an apprenticeship, Tomás." She chuckled. "But not as a clerk. Welcome to the Dragonseer Guild."

5
THE GUILD

"My name is Berin," said the woman. "I'm a dragonseer, like you, Tomás. Angus is my dragon." Berin's eyes twinkled. "Or perhaps I am his human."

Behind her, the huge shape of Angus nodded, then stretched downward. He and Berin leaned against each other, eyes closed. Berin's cheek rested on Angus's enormous jowl. Then the dragon sighed and grew dark, as if a light

had gone out, leaving him in shadow, deeper and deeper . . . until he was gone.

Berin opened her eyes.

"What happened?" asked Tom, amazed.

"Angus has returned to his world." Berin smiled. "It's easier this way—a thirty-foot dragon isn't easy to hide, after all!"

"So . . . they can go back?"

"Oh, yes. They can only enter our world when summoned, but they can leave whenever they like." She nodded to Malik, and they set off down a small side street.

"I don't understand," said Tom. "Why does nobody know about them?"

"The world of Draconis has changed," said Berin. "After the Dragon Storm, they almost

all returned home. They would not come back for centuries, no matter how we begged."

"Dragon Storm?"

Berin sighed. "A great battle. And a sad story, for another day. But now they are returning. A new breed of dragons, looking for new dragonseers. It's a very exciting time, young Tomás!"

Malik led them deeper into the old, dark city, through narrow streets and narrower lanes, to a small, hidden door. He glanced around and then ushered them through.

It was almost black inside, just shadows and dim shapes. Malik found another door, and another corridor, and more, leaving Tom bewildered. He heard metal and wood clunking around them like clockwork gears. The corridors seemed to move under their feet. . . . *How big was this building?*

Berin strode onward, and Tom had no choice but to keep up. At last they reached one more ancient doorway and entered.

Tom gazed around him in wonder.

He'd expected to see a room, or perhaps even to end up back outside. But instead, they were standing on a balcony that ran around the edge of a hall so vast that he could hardly see the other side. Globes of strange white light shone from above. Below them were a training ground and buildings, like a little village. People called to each other with tiny, echoing voices.

And in the air, dragons flew.

"Oh!" Tom gasped. There were different types! Some dragons were long and thin, with wispy tails. Others were powerful, beating their wings like eagles. There were large dragons as well as small and nimble ones. They soared between the globes, swooping

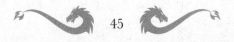

and turning. And each one carried a rider—
a human!

"Welcome, Tomás," said Berin. "Welcome
to the Dragonseer Guild."

Tom shook his head, astonished. "Where
are we? There's no building this big in all of
Rivven! Are we still in the city?"

Berin laughed. "In a way. Come."

She led Tom down a stairway to the
ground. "This is our home," she said.
"You'll live here and train here. You'll
learn about dragons and summoning."
She waved upward, to the dragons sailing
through the air. "And flying and how to
look after them."

She walked toward a low building and

ushered Tom inside. He found himself in a long room, near a table piled up with food—fresh bread, cheese, bowls of fruit, a huge pot of thick bean stew. It was noisy, full of chatter and squabble, and as they entered, a group of boys and girls looked up.

"Students!" called Berin. "We have a new recruit! Tomás, these are your fellow apprentices." To the others, she said, "Introduce yourselves and make a space. I'll see you all tomorrow. Good night!"

With that, she gave Tom a smile and a wink. Then she left, closing the door behind her.

Tom turned and stared at the group. "Er . . . ," he said.

"Hello!" A tall, wide-shouldered girl

strode forward and shook Tom's hand with a powerful grip. She examined him. "Strong shoulders. Blacksmith's boy?"

Tom blinked. "Um, yes."

"I'm Erin," said the girl. "Welcome to Hut Three. I'm in charge here."

"No you're not!" shouted the others.

Erin glowered. "Well . . . I should be. I was here first!"

A boy stood up, pale-skinned with curly red hair. "Connor," he said. "And actually, as I know most about dragons, I'm in charge."

"Rubbish!" snapped Erin.

"Am so!"

They started arguing, ignoring Tom.

"I'm Ellis," said another boy. Ellis had rich

dark-brown skin, black hair, and a curious expression. He held a large piece of parchment. "Where are you from?"

"Tern Hill," said Tom, and the boy drew a careful mark. Tom realized the parchment was a map.

"You're a blacksmith?" asked another girl.

Tom nodded. "Well, my dad is—"

"Good! I'm Mira. What do you know about tensile strength in copper cables?" The girl stared at him. She had grease on her face, and her long hair was tied with an oily rag.

"Um—"

"I am in charge!" bellowed Erin.

"Tern Hill off Tin Street, yes?" called Ellis.

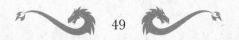

"Or what about shear effect?" insisted Mira, holding up a strange mechanical contraption. "It's for a steering harness, see?"

Tom blinked.

"You can't be in charge; you can't even do summoning—"

"But—"

"QUIET!"

For a moment, everyone stopped. A short, slim boy with black hair grinned at Tom. "Give the poor lad a break. I'm Kai. We're having dinner. Hungry?"

Tom's stomach growled. "Starving."

"Help yourself," said Kai. "Welcome to the Guild."

Tom sat down, smiling. "Thanks!"

Kai leaned forward. "Also . . . I'm in charge."

"WHAT? No way!"

"It's definitely not you, Kai!"

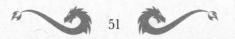

After supper the boys showed Tom their dorm room. That night he lay awake in the dark—warm, full of food, and in a comfortable bunk with fresh sheets.

Better than straw beds and thin soup, he thought, remembering Dad's words. He grinned. Dad hadn't imagined this!

Then he sighed. He'd been in such a whirl he hadn't thought about his parents. What would they say? What would he tell them? Suddenly he felt very homesick. Right now he'd be settling down in his tiny bed, in their little cottage. . . .

"Good night, Mom," he whispered. "Good night, Dad."

He lay in the dark, thinking about home and wondering what tomorrow might bring.

6
SUMMONING

Breakfast was in the hut the next morning, and just as loud as dinner was the night before. Voices clamored, plates clattered, arguments flared, and today a woman in a white apron was holding a huge frying pan and chatting to the children.

"Ah, the new recruit," she boomed when Tom and Kai entered. "Sausage? Eggs? Bacon, toast, mushroom, roast tomatoes?"

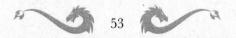

Tom stared at her. "Um . . . yes, please!"

The woman piled food onto a plate for him. "There, that'll get you started. I'm Hilda. Eat up!"

The food was delicious. Tom looked around as he ate. Everyone was there. Erin, the athletic girl, was arguing with Mira about her dragon harness. Kai and Connor had opened a pile of books and were discussing them. Ellis was redrawing his map, his tongue sticking out slightly in concentration. And there was one other girl, with white-blond hair and a sharp nose, eating alone. Kai said her name was Cara, but that she kept to herself. She glanced up as Tom looked around. He gave her a nod, but she turned away.

"Listen up!" bellowed Hilda. "Boys' turn to do the dishes today—come on! Training starts at eight."

They cleared up under Hilda's watchful eye and headed to the training ground. Berin was there, talking to two other adults: a man wearing gray robes and a short woman in bright yellow.

"Good morning!" Berin said to Tom. "Let me introduce you. This is Daisy, our self-defense instructor, and Vice Chancellor Creedy. Daisy, Vice Chancellor, this is Tomás, our newest recruit."

The woman gave Tom a wide, happy smile and bobbed her head.

However, the man glowered at him. "Oh, yes. The blacksmith's boy." His lip curled. "What's next, Chancellor—pig farmers?"

Tom didn't know what to say.

Berin frowned. "The dragon chose Tomás. He has every right to be here."

"And how am I supposed to teach a boy who's happier holding a hammer than a pencil?" the man sneered.

"That's not—" started Berin, but Tom interrupted.

"I can manage both, actually!" he snapped. "I mean . . ."

Creedy snorted. "No self-control, of course."

He shook his head. "Well, I'm sure you know what you're doing, Chancellor. I have work to do. Good day." He marched away.

Berin sighed. "Please forgive Creedy," she said. "He's rather . . . old-fashioned."

Tom felt his face turn red and wished that he hadn't shouted.

"Anyway," continued Berin, "come with me, Tomás." She nodded to Daisy and led Tom away. Behind them, the other children began hitting practice dummies with sticks. The air filled with the sounds of thwacks and cracking wood.

"Why do we need self-defense?" asked Tom as they walked.

Berin sighed. "It is wonderful to be chosen by a dragon. But these days, sadly, it is also dangerous. People are scared of dragons. Sometimes scared people lash out."

Tom remembered the fear in his mom's voice when he'd asked about dragons.

"That's why we formed the Guild," Berin continued. "Dragons are returning to the land, but they're still weak. We bring young dragonseers here to teach them and their dragons how to survive. We also hope to teach them how to help others. But for now we must stay hidden. We must tell no one. Not even your parents."

Tom didn't like the sound of that. He hated the thought of lying to Mom and Dad, or keeping secrets from them.

"Here we are."

They had reached a round stone building, with a chimney and two enormous doors. Inside, a man was piling wood into a firepit. He wore a brown leather jerkin, and his wrinkled face was hidden under a shaggy gray beard. He beamed at them.

"Hello!" he roared, grasping Tom's hand. "Tomás, yes? Pleased to meet you! Lookin' forward to seein' it, eh?"

Tom blinked. "What?"

"Why, your dragon, of course!" He laughed. "I'm Drun. I'll teach you how to summon."

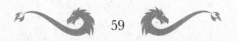

DRAGON STORM

Drun closed the doors and led Tom toward the firepit.

"A blacksmith's boy like you knows about fire, I assume," he said. "But you still need to be careful. Sit back here." He sat on the other side of the pit and watched Tom through the flames. Berin waited silently in the shadows.

"Look into the fire, Tomás," he said. "Relax. Watch the flames."

Tom did so and Drun nodded. "Good. Now, tell me about the first time you saw the face. What was it like?"

Tom thought back. "It was black," he said.

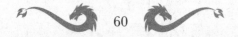

"And long, with ridges . . ." He described the face and how its eyes had burned.

Drun gazed at him. "Again," he whispered. "Everything you remember."

Tom described it again, watching the flickering flames. And suddenly he saw something—a black speck in the heart of the fire! A shimmer. A shape. A face with a bony crest and burning eyes . . .

"Slowly now," said Drun.

"Is it . . . real?"

Drun chuckled. "*Real*'s a difficult word, lad. Just watch and remember. How did it feel? No, don't tell me. Hold it in your head. . . ."

Tom remembered the way the face had

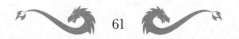

stared at him. It had been terrifying. And yet somehow good, too.

"Nearly there . . . ," Drun muttered.

It felt hot inside the room. The flames

rose out of the firepit and turned red, then white-hot. They roared! Tom stared,

forgetting everything except the face, the face in the fire. . . .

And then the fire collapsed and went out, and everything became black.

Tom gasped. "What happened?"

"Shh," whispered Drun. "Quiet, now. Absolutely still."

Tom realized there was something else in the room.

He froze. He sensed a large, dark shape behind him, uncoiling, stretching. There was a whisper of movement and a slither of leathery skin. Then a snort and hot breath on the back of his neck.

"Ah," said Drun happily. "There you are."

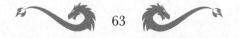

7
IRONSKIN

Tom turned and faced his dragon.

It was twice as tall as him, and long. Its skin was deep red, like weathered iron. But this wasn't a hard metal thing. It was alive. Thin lines of orange and yellow ran along its body like cracks, glowing as if a fire burned inside.

It sat like a cat, with its back legs curled and front paws on the dirt floor, claws digging into the earth. A thick tail swept behind it, and a

long neck stretched upward. Its forehead was bony and ridged, just like he'd seen in the flames, and its eyes gleamed.

It stared at Tom, leaning its head slightly to one side, and he stared back.

"What a beauty," murmured Drun.

"Can it . . ." Tom gulped. "Can it talk?"

The dragon made a deep rasping sound and opened its mouth to reveal huge white teeth. "Oh, yes," it said in a rumbling voice. It sounded amused. "And I'm a she, not an it."

She studied him. "You are . . . Tomás," she said. "And I . . ." She frowned, gazing down as if seeing herself for the first time. "I am . . . Ironskin. Yessssss . . ."

Berin stepped forward. "In their world,"

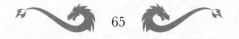

she said, "dragons are more like . . . an idea. A dream of dragons. Their shape, like their name, comes when they first arrive here."

"It comes from you, lad," said Drun. "Every dragonseer sees something different."

"You're like the forge at home," murmured Tom.

Ironskin stretched her paws. "This is a good form," she said. "I feel strong. I like it."

"And she'll change again too, when she gets her powers," said Drun.

"Powers?" asked the dragon, sounding interested. "What powers?"

Drun grinned. "I'm not sure. Every dragon's different. But they'll be somethin' you need, and they'll appear when you need them."

Tom gazed up at her.

"Now, Tomás," said Drun. "I can help you summon her until you get the hang of it. But there's somethin' you got to do yourself. Now she's here, you got to help her stay."

Tom frowned. "What do you mean?"

Berin said, "The bond between a dragonseer and their dragon is the power that holds them to this world, Tomás. Can you sense it?"

Tom looked up into Ironskin's face, and she peered down. As he looked, he realized that he *could* feel her. It was like a shape in his heart that he hadn't noticed before, but which had always been there. It felt right.

Ironskin grinned. "Thank you, Tomás."

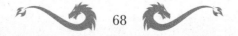

"Well done, lad," said Drun. He clapped his hands. "So! Shall we go and meet the others?"

Drun pulled open the large doors, and Ironskin peeked out into the world of the Guild Hall. She blinked in the light of the lanterns and padded forward.

"Walking feels good." She chuckled in a deep, throaty rumble. "The light feels good. Everything smells good. I like your world, Tomás!"

Berin and Drun led them back to the training ground, where the others had finished their self-defense lesson. Creedy was there, and he gave Ironskin an appraising stare. But the other children ran toward Tom, cheering.

"You got your dragon!" shouted Erin.

Tom grinned. "She's called Ironskin."

"Wow!" breathed Ellis. "She's fantastic!"

"Hello, Ironskin!" called Connor.

"Ironskin, these are my friends," said Tom.

Ironskin's lips curled into a smile and she bowed.

Kai pulled a string from one pocket and held it up against one of her back legs, writing measurements down in a notebook.

"Strong shoulders," he muttered. "Prominent brow ridges, elongated neck . . ."

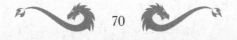

"When you're quite finished!" snapped a voice.

They looked up to see Creedy glaring at them.

"Find a space and summon your dragons," he ordered. "Those of you who need help"—his lip curled—"go to Drun."

The others spread out and closed their eyes. Erin, looking embarrassed, walked over to Drun, and they found a space together. Tom stayed where he was and watched.

There was a pause and a sharp tang in the air, like before a storm. And then, beside Connor, a shape started to form. Faint as a summer shadow at first, then thicker and stronger until it was solid. A dragon.

It wasn't like Angus or Ironskin. It had a long body but short legs and small wings. It was thin, almost like a snake. Its mouth was less full of teeth, and it had bright-blue eyes. The dragon curled around Connor as he spoke to it.

Beside Ellis a dark-green, middle-sized dragon reared its head. It had large ears and a sturdy body with strong leathery wings. Nearby, Kai's dragon was almost white, with a red flare on its chest and an intelligent glint in its eyes.

Cara, the girl who had sat by herself, summoned an odd, faded creature that was difficult to see. It was small and appeared to be the color of everything around it. Tom

realized that if he didn't stare hard at it, the dragon almost seemed to vanish.

Erin's dragon was enormous, with huge hind legs and a ridge of spikes along its back. It batted playfully at Erin with one paw, and she batted it back. Mira's dragon was a curious brown-and-bronze creature, with very angular features that made it look almost like a mechanical toy. She rubbed noses with it and laughed.

Ironskin and Tom stared at them all in amazement.

"They're like me!" purred Ironskin happily.

"Come on, don't dawdle!" snapped Creedy. "Get your harnesses on!"

The others led Tom across the training

ground to some chests filled with metal buckles and leather. The buckles were very worn and had clearly been used countless times before.

Drun walked across the training ground. "Each dragon is different, so the harnesses are adjustable. Here." He pulled out a bundle of webbing and laid it across Ironskin's back, fastening the buckles underneath. Ironskin looked curious.

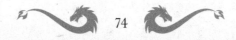

"Wait," said Tom. "Am I going to ride her? Like a horse?"

Drun laughed. "Dragons aren't horses. You remember that, lad, or you'll be in a world of trouble. But if you ask nicely, she might agree to carry you."

Creedy inspected every dragon, correcting and tightening, or making someone redo their buckles.

"Very well," he said at last. "Saddle up!"

The other children scrambled up the sides of their dragons and sat perched on top.

Tom looked at Ironskin. "Er," he said. "May I?"

Ironskin grinned. "Why not!"

So Tom, very carefully, climbed up the

harness. Ironskin's hide was warm and tough, and the orange and yellow streaks pulsed. He sat down and looked around him. It felt very high!

"Ready . . . ," called Creedy. "And trot."

The others started to trot in a circle.

"I think we're supposed to do the same," muttered Tom.

"How curious," murmured Ironskin. She moved forward, and Tom clutched at the harness as he swayed.

The dragons trotted around. *I'm riding a dragon*, thought Tom. *I'm riding a dragon.*

I'm riding a dragon!

8
THE RACE

"Sit up straight!" bellowed Creedy. "Guide with your knees!"

The dragons and their riders, all different shapes and colors, trotted around the training ground in a strange parade while their instructor glared at them.

"Why is that funny man shouting?" asked Ironskin loudly.

"Shh!" muttered Tom. "He's the teacher."

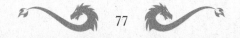

Behind them, Kai snickered.

"Keep control!" snapped Creedy.

Ironskin's body was strong, and Tom felt her huge shoulders coil as she trotted.

"This is fun," she hissed. "I like trotting. I like having muscles. I think I could go faster!"

Tom grinned and glanced around. Some of the other dragons also seemed to want to speed up, pushing their heads forward. The children were looking at Creedy as if waiting. He watched them all with a vague scowl of disapproval and finally sighed.

"Oh, very well. One lap around the hall. Go now!"

The neat order of the circle broke. All the dragons roared and raced toward the training

ground gate, jostling through and out. The children laughed and urged them on.

"No flying!" bellowed Creedy. He looked at Tom and Ironskin. "Well? What are you waiting for?"

Tom murmured, "Ironskin? Want to race?"

Ironskin roared—and charged!

Tom grabbed the harness as Ironskin's powerful legs bounded forward. "Running!" she snorted delightedly. "Running is good!"

The others had made for a dusty, churned-up racetrack that ran around the Guild Hall. They were ahead, almost at the first corner, but Ironskin soon caught up with Ellis's squat green dragon. It was ambling along, and as they overtook the pair, Tom saw Ellis gazing up at the hall, mindless of the race, making notes. Ironskin laughed, and her back feet scrabbled as she turned.

Connor, Erin, and Mira were leading, followed by Kai and then Cara, now just ahead of Tom! Cara's dragon, with its curious mottled pattern that seemed to blend into the background, was sleek and quick, but not as large as Ironskin. Tom and Ironskin overtook them just before the second corner. Tom grinned at Cara as they passed, but she didn't look up.

Ironskin ran in huge loping strides like a dog, bouncing Tom around until he found a stable place between her shoulders. They were catching up with Kai now. Kai's dragon was strong and sturdy, but Ironskin was faster!

"Come on, Boneshadow!" shouted Kai. "Come on!" He looked sideways at Tom and laughed as they passed. "Your dragon is fast!"

Tom grinned and held on as they turned the third corner. Now the leading group was closer. Mira's strange bronze-colored dragon was slowing. Mira was urging it on but it was getting tired, and Ironskin passed them easily. Ahead, Connor and Erin were racing neck and neck toward the final turn. Erin's huge dragon pounded the ground with every stride, but Connor's dragon—the thin, whip-like creature—was surprisingly fast. They charged at the corner, neither giving way— and collided!

"Argh!" shouted Connor, crashing to one side.

"Argh!" roared Erin, leaping and rolling clear. They started accusing each other. Tom and Ironskin slipped past them—and into the final stretch of the racetrack!

Tom risked a glance behind them and saw

TOM AND IRONSKIN

Kai and his dragon, Boneshadow, with its white body and bright-red-flared chest, still chasing. Ironskin was slowing now, her tongue lolling between her lips.

"Come on, Ironskin!" he roared. She sped up, but now Tom heard Boneshadow's paws thudding into the ground behind them, and Kai laughing. Tom started laughing too. Ironskin's back was hot, and the lines on her back were just like the fires of the forge. Tom gazed at them, and then he remembered helping Dad at home and working the bellows. He remembered his little room, and sitting at the table with Mom and Dad. . . .

Ironskin lurched.

DRAGON STORM

"Whoa!" shouted Tom.

For a moment, the dragon had almost seemed to fade. She stumbled and veered across the racetrack, her legs moving too fast to keep up with themselves. Kai and Boneshadow raced past them toward the line. Ironskin tried to recover but then lurched again, tripped, and crashed down. Desperately, Tom held on to the harness until the last moment, then hurtled clear. He slammed into the ground and shook his head.

"Ow!"

Turning back, he saw Ironskin looking at him with a surprised expression, and then . . . and then . . .

And then she faded out of sight and was gone.

"Ironskin?" he gasped, staring at where she had been. "Ironskin!"

Ahead of him, Kai and Boneshadow crossed the line and turned in triumph. Then they saw Tom. They trotted back, looking concerned.

"Tom, what happened?"

"She disappeared!" said Tom. "She was there, and then she disappeared!"

DRAGON STORM

The others were catching up now. Drun jogged across to join them.

"It's all right, lad," he called out. "You just lost your connection, that's all. She'll be fine."

"What are you standing around for?" came a harsh voice. Creedy arrived, glared at Tom and the others, and shook his head. "That's enough for today. Dragons, please return to your realm! Students, gather up harnesses and put them away neatly."

Tom realized that Ironskin's harness webbing was still lying on the ground where she had landed. As the other children murmured goodbyes, their own dragons faded away.

Drun put a hand on Tom's shoulder. "It's

fine, Tomás. She'll be back. We'll let her rest and call her again tomorrow. What did you think of her?"

Reassured, Tom grinned. "She's incredible!"

Drun beamed back. "That she is, lad. That she is."

9

SPACE IN
YOUR HEART

The next day, Erin and Tom reported to Drun's hut. Like Tom, Erin still needed help to summon her dragon, the enormous creature who called himself Rockhammer. Erin seemed embarrassed about it, but Drun cheerfully welcomed her inside. After a few minutes, the big doors opened again and Erin walked out with Rockhammer.

"See you at the training ground!" she called.

Then it was Tom's turn to enter the smoky darkness.

"Morning!" said Drun.

They took their places and went through the summoning ceremony again.

It was quicker this time. Tom looked into the flames and soon saw Ironskin's face, waiting there in his mind. And then she appeared, dark and magnificent, lined with fire, scratching at the ground as if eager to be off.

"Hello, Tomás," she growled happily. "I'm pleased to see you again."

Tom smiled and patted her, feeling the warm skin like stone on a hot day moving under his hand as she purred. The lines of orange and yellow glowed like the coals in the forge at home, and she was the color of old iron. Again it reminded Tom of working next to Dad, heaving on the bellows, feeling the scorching air around him.

"Tomás?"

Ironskin looked at him with a puzzled expression. To his horror, he realized that she was fading again!

"Ironskin!" he shouted. "Come back!"

"Tomás!"

Soon she was just a ghost, a shape in the air, just her eyes and a hurt expression, and now . . .

"Ironskin!"

Gone.

"Huh," muttered Drun.

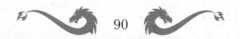

TOM AND IRONSKIN

Tom spun around. "What's happening?" he demanded.

Drun frowned. "Don't know," he said. "Seem to be having trouble with the bonding." He peered at Tom. "You can feel her, right? In your heart?"

"Yes! I felt her!" Tom blinked. "But . . . but then I saw her, and I thought about the forge at home. And . . ."

"Hmm," said Drun.

He took Tom to see Berin. She was at the training ground with Creedy. The other children were there with their dragons, and they stared at Tom in surprise. Drun explained the problem, and Berin gazed at Tom.

"Let's take a walk," she said.

She led him away from the grounds. For a while she was quiet.

"You miss your parents," she said at last.

Tom blinked. "Yes."

"Everyone does, of course. But some more than others. And Ironskin reminds you of home."

He nodded and they walked on.

"The life of a dragonseer is hard," said Berin. "To form a bond with your dragon, you have to hold her in your heart. You have to make space in your heart." She glanced at him. "Sometimes, that means letting go of other things."

Tom frowned. "What?"

"I mean . . . you may have to make a choice." Berin sighed. "For you as a dragonseer, your dragon must become the most important thing in your life. More important even than your home. Perhaps even your family."

Tom stared at her, aghast. "But I can't do that! Mom and Dad? I . . . I can't!"

She nodded. "No," she said sadly. "I'm sorry, Tomás. This may not be a choice you can make."

She had led them in a circle, and now they

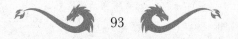

were returning to the grounds. Berin walked ahead and spoke to Creedy. He looked at Tom, his face blank. Then Berin returned.

"We'll try again tomorrow," she said. "Perhaps things will change. I'll talk to Drun and see what he can suggest."

She smiled at him, then headed off to Drun's hut.

"Class!" called Creedy. The children, who had been playing with their dragons, turned to face him. He glared at them.

"Today we will be practicing flight," he said. The students chattered excitedly, and he frowned. "No talking! Take your places."

He looked at Tom. "If you have no dragon,

you shouldn't be in this class. Return to your dormitory."

Tom nodded miserably. "Yes, sir."

"And, boy?" continued Creedy icily. "Summoning is one thing. But if you cannot form a bond with your dragon . . . then you are not a dragonseer."

Creedy turned away and started barking orders. Tom returned to the dorm and lay on his bunk. He thought about Ironskin and the feel of her as they had raced down the track. He thought of his life at home and in the smithy.

How could he choose? he wondered, staring at the ceiling. How could he possibly choose?

10
HOME

Every morning, Tom reported to Drun and
they summoned Ironskin. Each time she
appeared, she greeted Tom with a warm
growl, and he would reach out to her. Each
time, the warm iron of her skin and the
orange stripes of flame reminded him of
home, and memories of Mom and Dad
crowded into his head. And each time,

Ironskin, with a puzzled and hurt look on her face, faded away, and Drun sighed.

He patted Tom's shoulder. "We'll get there, lad," he said. "Don't worry."

But Tom did worry. The other children stopped asking him how he was getting on. They could see he was upset and they didn't know what to do.

Creedy wouldn't allow him at the dragon training, but Daisy, the self-defense instructor, didn't mind at all.

"Always useful to know self-defense, whatever happens," she trilled. "Find a space and join in."

He enjoyed her classes. Daisy wore bright-yellow leggings and tops. A pink ribbon was tied in her blond hair, and she spoke in a soft, breathless voice. At first, Tom wondered how someone so small could teach them to fight, until he saw her throw Erin halfway across the training ground. When fighting, Daisy bounced like a rubber ball and deflected attacks like magic.

"Strong shoulders," she said approvingly to him one day. "Blacksmith's shoulders, eh?"

"Yes," he said.

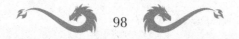

That night, lying awake, he thought about this. Blacksmith's shoulders. *Yes. I'm a blacksmith's son, and when I grow up I'll be a blacksmith. Or I'll run the market, like Mom. That's what I'll do. That's what I am. Not a dragonseer. That's not me.*

That was it, he realized. Ironskin was glorious, and he loved her. But how could he be a dragonseer if it meant giving up his family? Creedy was right—this wasn't his place.

I'm not a dragonseer.

And suddenly, Tom decided to go home.

He packed his bag and crept out of the dorm, into the Guild Hall. It was dark, the

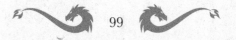

globes above as dim as stars as he climbed up to the exit. To his surprise, the door was already ajar, and he slipped out into the corridor. Leaving seemed simpler than arriving, the turns and passages obvious from this direction, and soon he was in the cold night air of Rivven.

He looked around. He wasn't sure where he was, and there was no building nearby that could possibly be large enough to be the Guild Hall. He wandered around the palace rock until he stumbled onto a street he recognized. He heard voices. He stopped, then crept forward and saw two figures talking. One was hidden in deep shadow . . . but the other was Vice Chancellor Creedy.

Tom gasped and pulled back. Were they looking for him already? But then he remembered the open door. Creedy must have left the hall earlier. As Tom watched, they seemed to finish their conversation. The other figure slipped away into the shadows, and Creedy turned back. Moonlight caught his face. He was scowling. Tom stood still, hardly breathing, as he stalked away.

What was Creedy doing? he wondered. It was late to be out—the city was asleep. But then Tom shook his head.

It wasn't anything to do with him. He wasn't a dragonseer. He hurried on toward home, but then—

There was a shriek!

Tom jumped. It was a horrible, vicious sound, full of fury—not human—somewhere close. A fire erupted from the roof of a nearby building! Another shriek sounded, and more flames billowed out. More buildings had caught fire up ahead.

Buildings on his lane.

He raced through the streets of Rivven. Now he heard panicked shouting. He smelled the sharp, harsh scent of burning and saw a haze of smoke in the air. The buildings were mostly wood, and the fire spread quickly. Men and women rushed out of their homes, dragging children. They formed lines of buckets and started passing water up from the well and throwing it onto the flames.

Tom ran to the lane where his parents lived and gasped. Everything was ablaze! The fire was out of control, the smithy roof was burning, and their tiny cottage was much worse. The air crackled and sparked, and the heat on his face was like a red wall, pushing him back.

"Mom!" he shouted. "Dad!"

Voices called to him from inside the cottage.

"Tomás?"

"Tom! Stay back!"

The front door crashed open, and he saw his parents trying to get out. Suddenly a huge

wooden beam collapsed, blocking their way, and a burst of sparks forced them back inside.

"Mom!" he howled. "Dad!"

"Tomás!"

They were trapped!

11
FIRE

"Mom!" Tom roared again. "Dad!"

The cottage blazed in front of him. There was no way in! He looked around for help but the whole street was on fire, and the adults were at either end, trying to keep the flames from spreading.

The air thundered and crackled. It was so fierce! What could possibly have caused it?

He stared in anguish at the flames. "Mom!"

I can help.

Tom jumped. The voice was inside his head! And then he saw something in the fire— a dark shape with a bony ridged forehead and burning eyes.

"Ironskin?" he croaked. "Is that you?"

I can help, Tomás. Summon me. I can help!

Was it possible? Perhaps Ironskin could make it into the cottage. . . .

"But I've never summoned you by myself!" he shouted.

You can do it.

Tom glanced around. No one had noticed him. He tried to remember Drun's lessons.

Look into the fire. Relax. He gazed at the flames. He tried not to think about his parents. He tried not to think about anything except Ironskin. It must be possible. The others could do it.

But you're not a dragonseer like the others, he thought.

Tom shook his head and tried again. He had to. He remembered Ironskin's claws digging into the ground, eager to leap. He remembered her skin like weathered iron, the way she stretched her forelegs, and her hot breath on the back of his neck.

"Tomás," growled a voice in his ear. "Well done."

Tom spun around and stared into the face

of Ironskin. She nodded her huge head. Tom hugged her hard but then stepped back. There was no time!

"Help them!" he shouted. "They're inside!"

Ironskin glared at the flames. "Yessssss . . ."

She padded forward. The fire didn't seem to worry her, but as she moved away from him, she grew dark again. She was fading!

Tom groaned and ran toward her, feeling the heat against his face like a slap.

"Not this time!" he roared. "Stay with me,

Ironskin!" He pressed his cheek against her warm, dry skin. "Stay with me!"

Ironskin stopped fading and snapped back into the world.

"I am staying," she growled. "But you must keep close."

"The fire's too hot!"

Ironskin nodded. She lowered her head, closed her eyes, and made a sound like the deepest purr Tom had ever heard, her whole body vibrating. She seemed larger, more powerful, and when she turned toward him, her eyes were clear.

The air around them grew cool. The fire was still raging—flames were everywhere!—but near Ironskin, a layer of cold protected Tom.

"Is this—"
Tom gasped.
The air was
clear as well,
no longer full
of bitter smoke.
"Is this your power?"

Ironskin nodded.
"Keep close."

She stepped into the flames with Tom by her side.

They reached the front door, and Ironskin batted the burning beam out of the way with her snout. Inside, the room churned with black smoke.

"There!" shouted Tom, pointing. His

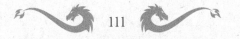

parents were lying on the floor, next to the back window, unconscious.

Tom remembered something Dad had told him about fires.

The smoke is worse than the flames, he'd said. *If you breathe it, you'll faint and never get out. Remember that, son. If you ever get trapped in a fire, try to stay low, out of the smoke.*

"They've fainted!" he shouted. "We'll have to carry them!"

The fire was getting worse. With a crash, the doorway behind them collapsed.

Tom tried to think. "The window!"

Ironskin lumbered across to Tom's parents, opened her huge mouth, and carefully scooped up Mom's body. Tom pushed the shutters open, and Ironskin leaned out and dropped Mom gently outside. Then she did the same with Dad.

"Well done!" cheered Tom. He started climbing through the window himself, but there was another crash, and he staggered back just as more beams collapsed around them.

They were cut off!

"Get on my back," hissed Ironskin.

Tom stared at her, then scrambled onto her back. Ironskin smashed at the roof beams with her head until they gave way, revealing open sky. Then she curled her hind legs and leaped straight up.

"Arrrgh!" yelped Tom.

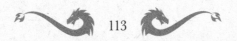

"Hold on!" growled Ironskin.

Tom didn't need telling! He wrapped his arms tightly around her and closed his eyes as they lifted, then started to fall.

He opened one eye. They weren't falling.

They were flying.

"Oh!"

Ironskin's wings had unfurled, thin and leathery, rippling in the air. They were thirty feet above the earth, lifted by the hot air from the flames below.

"Ahhhhhhh," murmured Ironskin. "So this is flying. Wonderful!"

Tom stared down at the houses and people fighting the fires. Farther off, tiny dots of light from lanterns flickered across the city, like stars in the night sky. It was beautiful, he thought.

"What's that?" he asked.

Ahead of them, moonlight glinted against metal. Tom realized he could make out something else—something large and leathery, flapping.

"Hey!" he shouted.

It spun around, seeming to notice them for the first time, and shrieked in rage. It was the same sound Tom had heard before! Then the creature raced away.

Ironskin snarled, beat her wings hard, tipped forward, and chased.

"Arrrgh!" yelped Tom again.

The wind whipped over his face. The shape in front banked to the right, and Ironskin followed. It was huge and fast, its heavy shoulders powering through the night air. A rider sat on its back, wrapped in a dark cloak, urging it on.

"It's another dragon!" roared Tom.

They raced across the sky. Now they were at the palace rock, and the creature rode the air currents upward, climbing steeply. It curled around the rock, and Ironskin chased, and then, and then . . .

And then it was gone.

Tom gasped. "Where did they go?"

Ironskin sniffed at the air. She cast back and forth, trying to find a trace. But somehow the creature had disappeared, just under the shadow of the palace walls.

"Gone," she hissed.

Tom realized they were near the walls themselves. "Come on," he said, patting her side. "We should go, before the guards see us."

Ironskin sniffed again, disappointed. Then she turned and flapped away, toward Tom's home. Mom and Dad were still lying on the ground, away from the flames. Ironskin swooped down, circled, and dropped, stretching her wings wide at the last moment, landing on all four legs like a cat.

Tom scrambled off Ironskin's back. "Mom!" he yelled. "Dad! Can you hear me?"

Mom groaned, and Dad started coughing.

He stared at Tom. "Tomás? Tomás!"

Mom was awake too. "I thought . . . The fire!" She tried to sit up.

"It's okay!" said Tom, holding her. "Everything's okay."

"Tomás!" roared Dad. "Behind you!"

He stumbled to his feet and dragged Tom

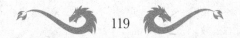

backward. "Run, boy! Take your mother! Run!"

Tom gaped at him. "What? What's wrong?"

And then he realized.

"Oh," he said. "Right. Dad, there's something you should know. . . ."

Ironskin dipped her head and gave a huge smile, showing all her teeth.

"Good evening," she purred.

12
WHATEVER
YOU ARE

Mom and Dad stared at Ironskin.

"It's okay!" said Tom. He stood in front of them. "Um . . . Mom, Dad . . . this is Ironskin."

"Pleased to meet you," said Ironskin.

Mom and Dad kept staring.

"She's a dragon," said Tom helpfully.

Dad glanced at Tom and then back to the enormous creature. His mouth fell open.

"Oh, I should probably explain." Tom scratched his head. "Um . . ."

But before he could say more, there was the sound of running footsteps and a man raced into the courtyard. He saw Ironskin and skidded to a halt.

"What are you doing?" he gasped.

It was Malik! He looked like he'd been fighting fires. He was covered in sweat and soot, and his voice was rough. "You can't be out in the open!"

Dad looked at Malik and then pointed one hand, rather shakily, at Ironskin.

"It's a dragon," he said. He sounded a little dazed.

"Captain Hork's almost here!" snapped Malik.

Suddenly Tom realized what he meant. He turned to Ironskin. "You have to go!" he said. "Do you understand?"

"Yes," murmured Ironskin. "I don't want to, though."

Tom smiled. Despite the fire still raging and the chaos around them, he felt a wave of happiness when he looked at her.

"Don't worry," he said. "It won't be for long, I promise."

Ironskin nodded and ducked her head. She grew darker and darker, covered in shadows, and was gone.

"What's going on here?" demanded a braying voice.

Tom turned. Captain Hork was on his horse, looking very cross. His helmet-plume feathers were singed and wilting.

"Captain, I was just investigating—" started Malik.

"Why aren't you putting out the fire?" barked Hork. "You're just standing around!"

Dad shook his head. "Yes," he muttered. He looked at his burning house as if he'd only now noticed it, and ran to the water pump. Hork's soldiers came forward and helped, and they formed a bucket chain, while Hork shouted orders at them from his horse.

They worked for hours, putting out the last

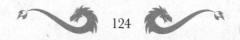

flames just before dawn. Tom collapsed to the ground. He was exhausted; his legs felt like jelly, and his lungs were full of smoke. When he glanced around the ruined courtyard, he saw Mom and Dad staring at him. He let his head fall to his chest, and he groaned. What could he say to them?

"You!" snapped Hork. "You caused this!"

Tom looked up. Hork was pointing a sword at Dad.

Dad stared in astonishment. "My lord?"

"Your forge must have got out of control!" shouted Hork. "Look at the damage you've done!"

Malik frowned. "Sir, I'm not sure that's the case. I believe the forge was out—"

"Nonsense! What else could have caused a fire this severe?"

"It's nothing to do with us!" protested Mom, but Hork ignored her.

"Guards, seize this man!"

Tom stumbled to his feet. What should he

do? Could he summon Ironskin again? But before he tried, a clear voice cut across the chaos.

"That won't be necessary, Captain."

Captain Hork turned in fury, then stopped.

Berin stood before him, smiling.

"My lady," he gasped. He bowed very low and almost fell off his horse. Feathers sagged over his face.

"Well done for putting out the blaze, Captain," said Berin. "But I can assure you, it wasn't caused by the forge."

"But . . . ," Captain Hork spluttered. "My lady, of course I would not doubt you, but what else could it be?"

"Lightning," said Berin.

Captain Hork blinked. "Lightning?"

Berin nodded. "I saw it myself."

Hork hesitated. He glanced up at the early-morning sky, clear and fine and completely empty of storm clouds. He licked his lips nervously. "But . . ."

Malik stepped forward, smiling. "Well, thank you, Lady Berin, for clearing things up. I think that's all sorted, isn't it, Captain?"

Hork seemed about to protest, but then stopped. "Yes? Well . . . lightning. Yes." He glared at his men, sitting exhausted on the ground. "What are you doing, lying about?" he snarled. "On your feet!"

He bowed to Berin, turned his horse

around, and managed to make it trot away. The soldiers wearily trailed after him.

Malik nodded to Tom and his parents, grinned at Berin, and followed Captain Hork down the hill.

Berin watched them leave, then turned to Tom's mom and dad. "I believe I owe you an explanation," she said quietly. "Tomás, may I have a moment with your parents?"

Tom waited at one end of the courtyard while Berin talked with Mom and Dad. Occasionally, Mom or Dad, or both, stared at him. At one point, Mom's voice rose to a shout and then dropped to a fierce whisper.

After a while they walked back. Their faces looked serious.

"Lady Berin has told us . . . some things," said Dad carefully. "Are they true?"

Tom sighed. "Yes."

"But . . . a dragon?" Mom said.

He nodded. "Yes."

Dad thought. Then he clambered into the remains of the smithy, rummaged around, and pulled out a battered, blackened sword. A dragonsword.

He swung it from side to side, testing the balance. He examined the swirling markings and stared hard at Tom. "Right," he said.

He thrust the sword down between two rocks, wedging it tight. With one mighty heave, he bent the blade into a right angle. Then he pulled it free and threw the mangled hunk of metal across the courtyard, where it clanged loudly against the cobblestones.

"I'll make no more of these, then," he said.

Tom swallowed. "So . . . it's okay?"

Mom laughed. "Son, of all things, you know this: We love you, whatever you are. Even if what you are is . . . is . . ."

"Amazing," said Berin from behind them. "What he is, is amazing."

His parents nodded, and Tom grinned.

Berin looked around the courtyard, then at the ruined cottage and the forge. "What will you do now?"

"My sister can put us up for a bit," Mom said. "We'll cope."

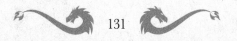

"I can repair the forge," said Dad. He smiled wryly. "Although there may be no point. There was money in dragonswords. I'm not sure what we'll do now."

Berin smiled. "I may have an idea," she said.

13

DRAGONSEER

Tom worked the bellows, blowing air into the
fire until it glowed a fierce yellow, while beside
him Dad hammered at a metal shape.

"Ready?" roared Dad.

"Yes!" Tom shouted. Dad
plunged the metal into the forge.
As always, he ignored the
heat and waited until
the shape softened,

then removed it and hammered the edges. He sank it into the water trough, and the air filled with the bubbling HISSSSSS! of steam. Finally, he held it up.

"There," he said. "That should do."

He placed it in a bag with the other pieces. "Good work, son."

Tom grinned.

"Tomás!" called Mom from outside. "Lady Berin is here."

Tom left the smithy and saw Berin standing in the courtyard, smiling and chatting with Mom.

"The repairs are going well," observed Berin. She nodded to the cottage. "You've done a remarkable job, Sofía."

Mom chuckled. "I've been organizing the neighbors, getting everyone to work together. They helped us rebuild the forge, and Felipe's been doing mending work for them. Among other things." She winked.

"Ah," said Berin. "And how are your extra projects going?"

Tom opened the bag and showed her the metal pieces. "They need polishing," he said. "But they're ready to go."

"My first dragon harness," mused Dad. "Isn't that something?"

Berin nodded in approval. "The first of many, Felipe." She handed him a small leather pouch, jingling with coins. "Here's to your new trade."

Tom hugged his parents and then headed down the hill with Berin. He looked back as he walked, waving to them until he and Berin went around a corner.

"Drun was very pleased to learn of Ironskin's powers," said Berin. "He says Protection magic is very rare."

"Is that what she has?" asked Tom.

Berin nodded. "She made the fire grow cold, and stopped you from choking on the smoke. She may be able to do more, too."

"If she hadn't . . . ," started Tom. He gulped. "I don't know what would have happened to Mom and Dad. Ironskin saved them."

Berin smiled. "The powers a dragon discovers in this world are linked to her dragonseer. They came from you. You both saved them, Tomás."

Tom thought about that. It was a nice feeling.

"And you held Ironskin in the world," continued Berin. She glanced at him. "So, have you made your choice?"

"Yes." Tom remembered Ironskin's glorious dark shape, and the red and yellow flame patterns. And he remembered the forge, and his home, and Mom and Dad. "I choose both."

Berin looked surprised.

Tom shrugged. "When Ironskin came, and she needed me to keep her there, I could feel her and my parents at the same time." He shook his head. "I can't explain it. Maybe there can always be space. Maybe the more things you put in your heart, the more space there is."

"Hmm," Berin said thoughtfully. "You know, Tom, I believe Ironskin was right to pick you."

They headed into the old town as the sun set over the city, casting it in an orange glow and long shadows. After a while, Tom said, "I saw something that evening. A dragon."

Berin nodded. "Ah . . ."

"We chased it, but it escaped near the palace." Tom hesitated. "I think it started the fire."

They walked on in silence.

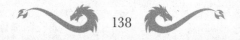

"It's not one of ours," said Berin at last. "I cannot tell what it is yet, but something is happening—or going to happen—soon. A Storm . . . We must do what we can to learn more. We must be watchful. I've asked Creedy to investigate."

Tom remembered seeing Creedy in the city that night. That must have been why he'd been talking to the shadowy figure. Creedy had been scowling—had he known the creature would strike? Tom shook his head. He sensed that Berin and Creedy knew something they weren't telling him, but for now, he would have to trust them. He trusted Berin. And Berin trusted Creedy. . . .

They strolled through the old city lanes until

they reached the doorway to the Guild. Berin led Tom inside, and once again he heard the curious clockwork sounds and felt the corridors shudder under his feet. The next thing he knew, he was at the edge of the Guild Hall.

Berin stopped. "Tomás, you don't have to return."

"I know."

Tom looked around at the training ground and huts and smiled. "But it seems like the right place. After all . . . I'm a dragonseer."

Berin smiled back.

As they reached Tom's hut, Erin and the other children burst out.

"Tom!"

"Where have you been?"

"We heard there was a fire!"

"Were you in a fight? Was there a fight?"

Even Cara, the silent girl, had emerged, standing by the door. When he noticed her, she hesitated, then nodded.

He nodded back. "Yes," he said. "I mean, no, no fight. But I chased a dragon! And . . ."

He turned to Berin. "Can I summon her?"

She beamed. "Certainly!"

Tom closed his eyes. It was so easy now. He remembered the fire, and saw Ironskin's face, and felt again the space in his heart that was hers. . . .

"Ironskin!" cheered the others.

Tom turned, and there she was, with her deep-red skin and veins of orange and yellow, and her ridged forehead.

"And . . ." Connor hesitated. "Can she stay?"

Tom smiled. "As long as she likes."

"You'll be able to join us for training!" said Kai. "You can learn to fly!"

Tom and Ironskin grinned at each other. Tom swung up and onto her back. Ironskin shook her head and growled in happiness.

"We might skip that part," he said.

Ironskin curled her hind legs like a spring and leaped into the air. . . .

And they flew.

THE DRAGON STORM IS COMING.

Soar into adventure with dragonseer
Cara and her dragon, Silverthief!

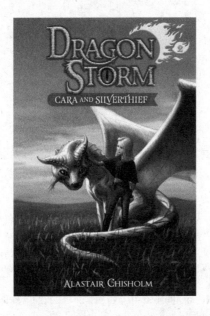

Turn the page for a sneak peek at
the next book in the Dragon Storm series!

THE SILVER THIEF

In the dead dark of a moonless night, a young girl climbed the palace walls.

The palace stood on an ancient rock that rose high above the city of Rivven. Its walls were well made, crafted from smooth gray stone with a few handholds. The girl moved confidently, ignoring the drop below her. Finding a crack between two stones, she pulled herself up and placed her feet onto a thin ledge. She reached for the next gap.

Wait.

The voice came from inside her head. She didn't know how or whose voice it was, but she'd heard it her whole life. It was her only friend, and she trusted it. She stopped. Above her, a guard leaned out over the edge of the wall and gazed down, bored. The girl waited, hidden in a gray cloak that perfectly matched the stonework, until the guard wandered away.

Now, said the voice.

She kept climbing until she came to a

narrow window about halfway up, then squeezed through and into a corridor, landing in a crouch. No one was around. Faint torchlight flickered at one end, and a solid wooden door blocked the other.

She removed her cloak and tucked it into her backpack. The girl was small and thin with silver-blond hair and a pinched, serious face. The dark colors she wore were mottled like shadows. She crept toward the door and listened for a moment, then slowly lifted the latch and entered.

Beyond were more corridors, some dark, some lit by torchlight. She moved cautiously. At one point, she stopped and sank into the shadows as a servant scurried past. The floor had rich red carpet now, and torches burned in alcoves.

On the left, said the voice.

The girl paused. The patch of wall to her left seemed different, the stonework slightly pale. She felt around the edges until she was sure, then pushed at one stone.

The wall swung outward, revealing a hidden entrance.

The girl's expression didn't change. She tiptoed into the darkness along a narrow passage, feeling her way until she reached another door, opened it, and entered a room.

Inside it was bright with lamplight. Every inch shone with precious metal, dark polished wood, and crystal. Beautiful embroideries covered the walls, shimmering with golden thread. In the middle of the room sat a huge four-poster bed.

This is it, said the voice. *King Godfic's royal quarters!*

The girl stared around, her mouth open.

Come on. We'd better be quick.

She nodded and tiptoed across to a grand dressing table in front of an enormous mirror.

He likes looking at himself, doesn't he?

The girl grinned and checked the drawers. One was full of little jars of powder and perfume. One held a display of embroidered lace handkerchiefs. One had papers and wax and the king's official stamp.

One was locked. The girl pulled two pins

from her hair and carefully used them to feel inside the lock. Then she *twisted,* and the lock clicked. She slid the drawer open and gasped.

The inside was lined with dark-red velvet, and its contents glittered. There were gold and silver rings, a heavy gold link necklace, and a chain of pearls. Beautiful, ornate pins were carved into the shapes of animals, inlaid with precious stones. Coins lay scattered at the base. And in the center, on its own stand, sat a large golden brooch with a grand diamond.

That's it!

Carefully, the girl picked up the brooch and examined it. The base was an octagon, with eight ornate golden sides, framing a diamond that shone like a star. There was something in the diamond's heart—or perhaps it was painted underneath? Peering closer at the diamond, she made out an eye, beautifully drawn, fierce, and somehow cruel. Not a human eye; more like a cat's, or a wolf's, or . . .

I don't like that.

"What?" The girl was surprised. "It's just a picture."

It's creepy.

She shrugged and looked back—and the eye moved.

"Argh!" she yelled, dropping the brooch to the floor. The eye glanced around, then straight at her, and blinked! Suddenly a bell started tolling from the corridor outside, hard and fast and sharp.

You've triggered an alarm!

"It moved!" she hissed.

I know! Forget it! Come on!

There were other noises now, shouts and running footsteps. The girl ran back to the far wall and the secret passage, closing the door behind her just as she heard someone at the main entrance.

She fumbled through the black corridor, trying to stay quiet. Would they know about the hidden entry? She reached the end of the passage and pushed the door open a crack. The corridor was empty, and she hurried back to where she'd come in, dragging her cloak and a grappling rope from her bag. She poked her head through the slit window, then pulled it back sharply and cursed. There were guards all along the top of the wall now, holding lanterns and searching intently.

We can't go that way—they'll see us!

The girl felt panic rise inside her. "Maybe—"

Boots thundered behind her. More guards!

She raced toward the brighter end of the corridor, back into the depths of the palace.

What are we going to do?

She kept moving, glancing around. There were rooms on either side. Could she sneak into one of them? The alarm bells clanged, and a guard shouted, "You check that way!"

What are we going to DO, Cara?

And then a black-gloved hand reached from a doorway, covered her mouth, and dragged her backward. The door closed behind her, and someone grabbed her arms and whispered harshly in her ear.